peg + cat

MATH IN THE BATH

A LEVEL 1 READER

JENNIFER OXLEY
+ BILLY ARONSON

CANDLEWICK
ENTERTAINMENT

Rock the Boat

Peg and Cat are
in the bath.

One Peg.
One Cat.
One, two friends
in the bath.

Peg and Cat do
math in the bath.

Peg and Cat have three rocks and one boat.

A small rock goes
in the boat.

A bigger rock goes
in the boat.

The biggest rock goes
in the boat.

Oh no! Where did the
rocks and boat go?

Too Many More!

One Pig is in the tub.

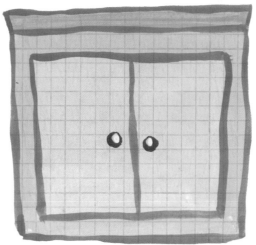

"More!"

says Cat.

Now one Pig and one
Cow are in the tub.
One, two in the tub.

"More!"

says Cat.

Now one Pig and one Cow and
one Hog are in the tub.
One, two, three in the tub.

Too many in the tub!

"Less!" says Cat.

Now there are zero
in the tub.

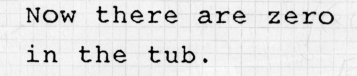

Path to the Bath

What is under the rug?

It's Bug!   And Worm!

Bug and Worm have a map.
Bug and Worm follow the map.

Bug and Worm go up.

Bug and Worm go across.

Bug and Worm jump
into the tub.

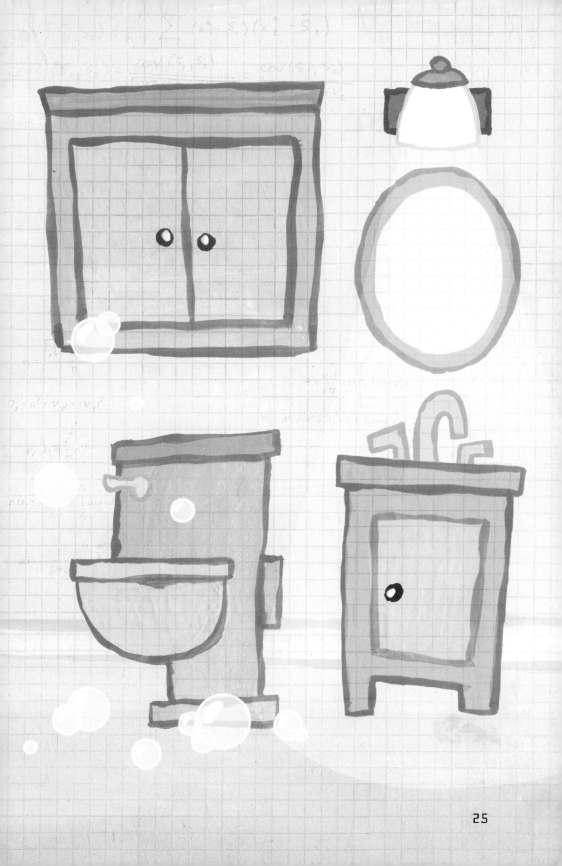

Bug and Worm are in the
bath. Peg and Cat are
in the bath.

One, two, three, four
friends in the bath.
Peg and Cat do math in
the bath.

This book is based on the TV series *Peg + Cat*.
Peg + Cat is produced by Fred Rogers Productions.
Created by Jennifer Oxley and Billy Aronson.
Math in the Bath is based on television background art by
Erica Kepler. Art assets assembled by Sarika Matthew.
The PBS KIDS logo is a registered mark of the Public
Broadcasting Service and is used with permission.

pbskids.org/peg

First edition 2019

Library of Congress Catalog Card Number pending
ISBN 978-1-5362-0699-9 (hardcover)
ISBN 978-1-5362-0700-2 (paperback)

18 19 20 21 22 23 APS 10 9 8 7 6 5 4 3 2 1

Printed in Humen, Dongguan, China

This book was typeset in OPTITypewriter.
The illustrations were created digitally.

Candlewick Entertainment
an imprint of Candlewick Press
99 Dover Street
Somerville, Massachusetts 02144

visit us at www.candlewick.com